This Pip and Posy book belongs to:

Based on the episode *Bug Hotel* by Andrew Emerson
Adapted by Lauren Holowaty

A Magic Light Pictures Ltd production in association
with Sky Kids, Channel 5/Milkshake! and ZDF.

First published 2023 by Nosy Crow Ltd
The Crow's Nest, 14 Baden Place, Crosby Row,
London, SE1 1YW, UK

Nosy Crow Eireann Ltd, 44 Orchard Grove,
Kenmare, Co Kerry, V93 FY22, Ireland

www.nosycrow.com

ISBN 978 1 83994 814 5

Nosy Crow and associated logos are trademarks and/or registered
trademarks of Nosy Crow Ltd.
Text © Nosy Crow 2023

www.magiclightpictures.com

Pip and Posy © Magic Light Pictures 2021

Pip and Posy is a registered trademark
of Nosy Crow Ltd and used under licence.

Licensed by Magic Light Pictures Ltd.

A CIP catalogue record for this book is available from the British Library.

Printed in China
Papers used by Nosy Crow are made from
wood grown in sustainable forests.

1 3 5 7 9 10 8 6 4 2

Pip and Posy™
The Bug Hotel

nosy crow

It was a lovely, sunny morning. Pip and Posy
were sitting on the roundabout at the playground.

"What do you call a roundabout for clouds?"
said Pip.

Posy shrugged. "A cloud-about!" cried Pip.

They both giggled.

"And a see-saw for a tree,"
began Posy, "is a tree-traw!"

Suddenly, they heard a voice . . .

It was their friend, Jamila.
Pip and Posy crept towards
Jamila to surprise her.

They tried to be quiet,
but they kept giggling.

Just as they got there . . .

Jamila spun round
to face them!

"AHHHH!"

they squealed.

"Shhh," hushed Jamila.
"Don't scare them."

"Scare who?" asked Posy.
She couldn't see anyone
else around.

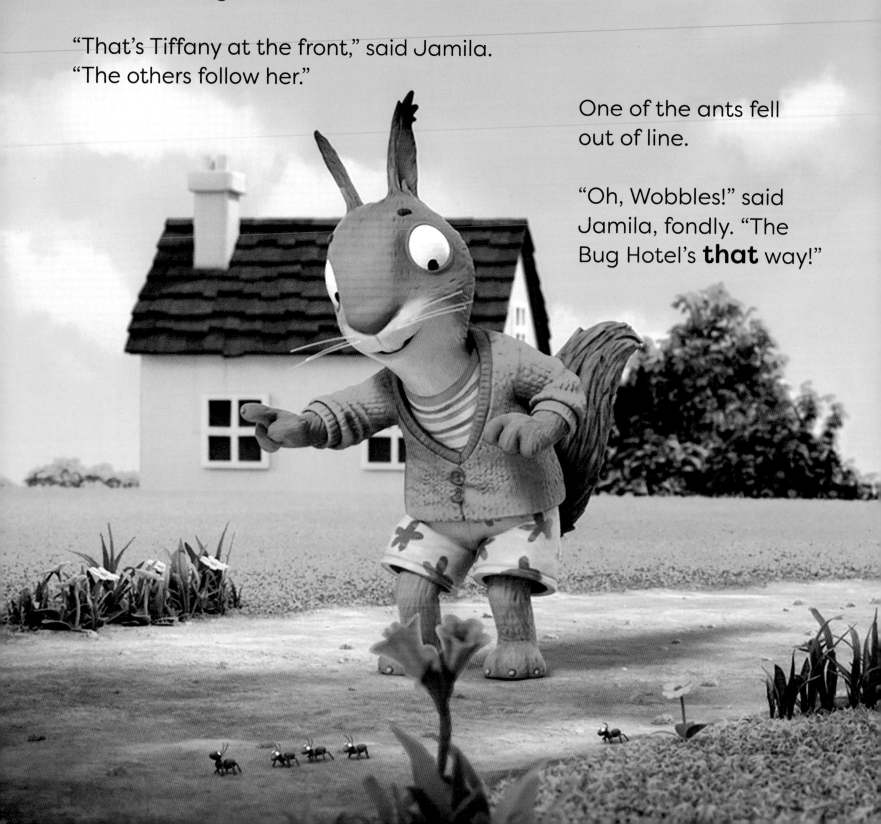

Jamila pointed to the path. Five little ants were marching in a line.

"That's Tiffany at the front," said Jamila. "The others follow her."

One of the ants fell out of line.

"Oh, Wobbles!" said Jamila, fondly. "The Bug Hotel's **that** way!"

"What's a bug hotel?" shouted Pip.

"Shhh!" whispered Jamila. "I'll show you."

Jamila led Pip and Posy along the path.
"Here it is," she said, proudly. "I made it myself."

"It's not a very big hotel," said Posy.

"That's 'cos it's for **bugs,**" said Jamila.

"There's a worm room –
he doesn't keep it
very clean.

A room for the beetles –
they squabble a **LOT!**

And that room's for the ladybird."

"It's like a **real** hotel!" said Posy.

Pip watched as a butterfly landed on the hotel roof.

"That's Cabbage, back from her morning flutter,"
said Jamila. "She lives on the top floor."

"But where are the ants
going to stay?" asked Pip.

"I'm going to make something specially for them," said Jamila.

"Can we help?" asked Posy.

"Yes, please! I need **lots** of twigs this long," said Jamila, holding out her hands.

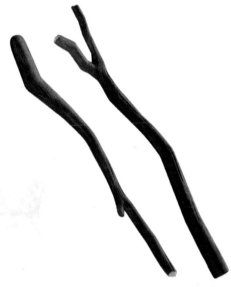

Jamila went off to find another cardboard roll to make a room for the ants.

"We'll find **heaps** of twigs for the ant room, Jamila!" said Pip as they waved goodbye.

"See you later, Jamila-bo-bila!" called Posy.

As Jamila skipped along the path, she spotted the ants marching towards the bug hotel.

"Not so fast, Tiffany," she said.
"Your room's not ready yet!"

Pip and Posy searched for twigs.

"Ooh, got one!" cried Posy, picking it up and balancing it on her nose.

"Got **two!**" cried Pip, using his to play air-drums!

Posy looked at the hotel. "Do you think the rooms are comfy?" she asked.

"Yes," said Pip. "I know because I'm the busy bee who runzzzzz the hotel!"

Pip buzzed around pretending to be a bee!

Bzz! Bzz! Bzz!

Posy flapped her arms. "And I'm Flappington the Butterfly!" she announced.

FLOOF! FLOOF! FLOOF!

All the noise made some of Jamila's
mini friends leave her bug hotel.

Cabbage flew off first.

Then the beetles hopped
down to the ground . . .

and the worm
wiggled away.

Only the sleepy
ladybird was left.

Pip and Posy were too busy playing loudly to notice.

"Do you do any sports at the hotel, Busy Bee?"
asked Posy, giggling.

"Yes! Let's play . . ." began Pip. "Moth-ball!"

Posy threw the ball to Pip, but it sailed over his head!

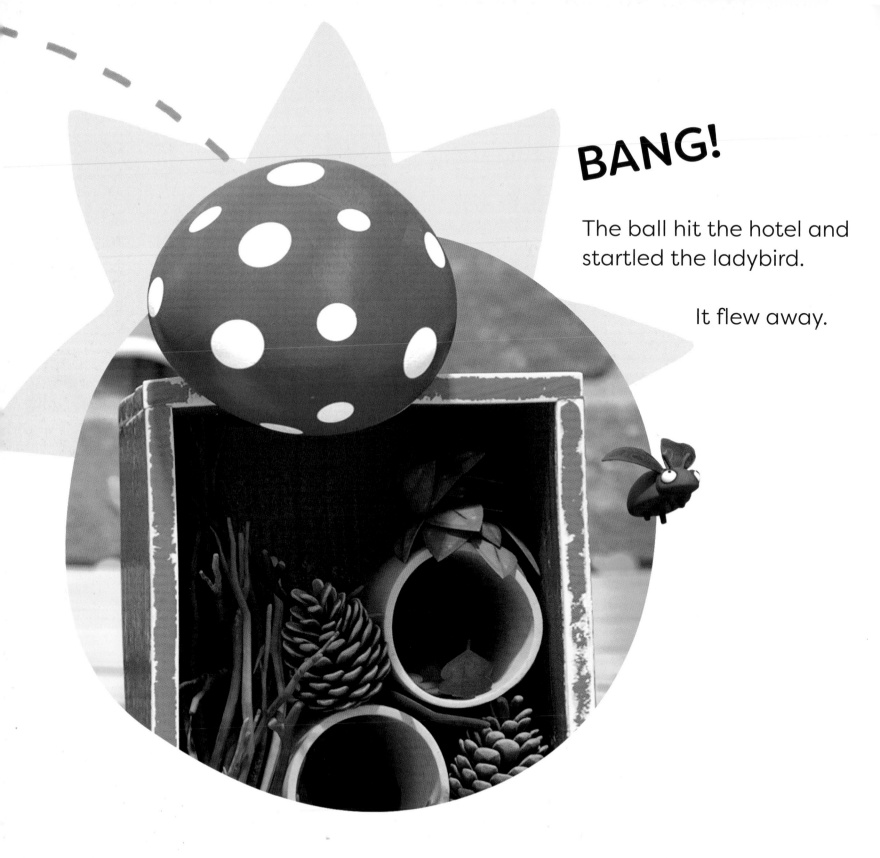

BANG!

The ball hit the hotel and startled the ladybird.

It flew away.

Now there were **no** mini friends left.

Then Pip threw the ball and it bounced on the path, right in front of the ants.

So the ants turned and marched back the other way.

But Pip and Posy didn't notice.

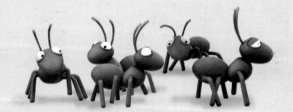

Jamila was skipping back
when she spotted the ants
going the wrong way.

"Tiffany?" she said. "The hotel's that way.
Look, here's your room."

Jamila heard loud giggling and ran over
to Pip and Posy.

"Have you got the twigs?" she asked. "I've got to make the ants' room. They're walking away!"

Pip and Posy showed Jamila the three twigs they had found.

"You said you'd get heaps," sighed Jamila. "I need more than three for . . ."

Jamila looked over at her hotel and saw that all the rooms were empty.

"All the bugs have gone!" she cried sadly.

"Have they?" said Posy, surprised.

"You were too noisy," said Jamila. "They've all moved out and now the ants are going away, too."

"Oh," said Pip and Posy, looking at each other.

"Let's turn them around," said Posy.

That gave Pip an idea . . .

He collected the three twigs and used them to make an arrow on the path that pointed back to the hotel.

"This way, ants!" he said.
"Ants don't know arrows," said Jamila.

But as Tiffany stepped onto a twig, Pip carefully swivelled it to turn her around.

"Watch," he whispered.

The other ants followed Tiffany onto
the twig and towards the hotel.

"Ooh!" said Jamila. "It's working!"

"We can lead them back," said Posy,
making a line of twigs.

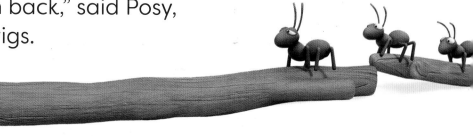

Pip and Posy spotted a puddle.
"Oh!" they gasped. But Posy had
a clever idea.

Jamila held her breath as
Posy made a twig bridge with
blocks and the ants crossed it
to safety.

Phew!

The twigs led the ants all the way to the hotel, where their cosy room was waiting.

"Ahhh, they **love** their twiggy, tubey room!" said Jamila, delighted.

The friends stayed very still and quiet, and a beetle scuttled back!

"HEYYY!" shouted Zac, popping up beside them.

"Shhh!" hushed Pip, Posy and Jamila. "Look."

Everybody watched
as something landed
on Zac's nose . . .

"Cabbage!" whispered Jamila.
"You came back."

It wasn't long before all the mini friends
had returned to the bug hotel.

"Hooray!" said everyone quietly.